My Must-Have MOM

Maudie Smith

 Lantana

My mom's not like most moms. Say there's a dumpster in the street, most moms will pass right by without a second glance.

Not my mom.

This book belongs to

....

NO LONGER PROPERTY OF SEATTLE PUBLIC LIBRARY

To Claire Hawcock, a must-have friend

Maudie

To my family and Harry, who taught me
to be courageous and follow my heart

Jen

First published in the United Kingdom in 2022 by Lantana Publishing Ltd.
www.lantanapublishing.com | info@lantanapublishing.com

American edition published in 2022 by Lantana Publishing Ltd., UK.

Text ©Maudie Smith, 2022
Illustration ©Jen Khatun, 2022

The moral rights of the author and illustrator have been asserted.
All rights reserved. No part of this publication may be reproduced,
stored in a retrieval system, or transmitted in any form or by any
means, electronic,mechanical, photocopying, recording or otherwise,
without the prior written permission of the copyright owner.

Distributed in the United States and Canada by Lerner Publishing Group, Inc.
241 First Avenue North, Minneapolis, MN 55401 U.S.A.
For reading levels and more information, look for this title at www.lernerbooks.com
Cataloging-in-Publication Data Available.

Hardback ISBN: 978-1-913747-71-8
eBook PDF: 978-1-913747-72-5
ePub3: 978-1-913747-73-2

Printed and bound in Europe
Original artwork created in pencil, colored digitally.

"Look at this, Jake!" she'll shout. "We must have this! We must have this, too! And we simply *must* have this!"

That's my mom for you. She's a must-have mom.

It's the same wherever we go.
Mom can't resist a good rummage.
Because where most people
see Trash and Junk, she sees
Opportunity and Treasure.

When Mom sees something she must have, we carry it back to our block. I press the buttons and up we ride to our apartment on the fourteenth floor.

We pass Mr. Price. We say hello, and he says,

"Harumph!"

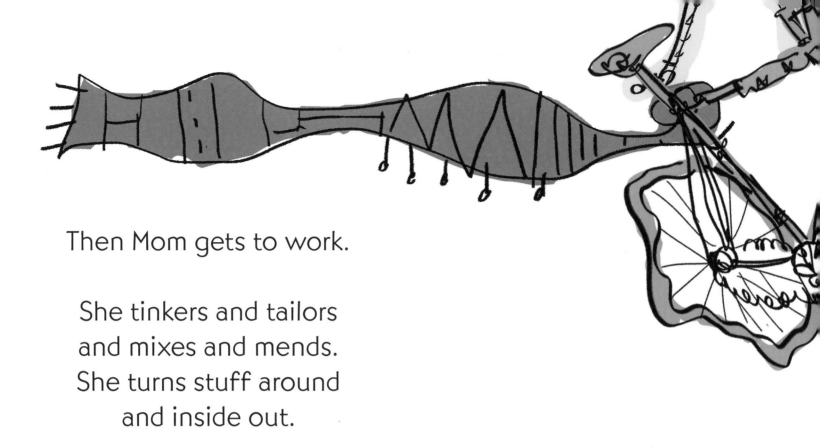

Then Mom gets to work.

She tinkers and tailors
and mixes and mends.
She turns stuff around
and inside out.

Mom can make something
new out of any old thing.

A bendy bike or a broken
bath. Tires and teapots,
traffic cones and jelly
jars. Lonely old cymbals
that don't even ring.

Once, we found a damp bedraggled rat . . .

And Mom turned that into quite a decent dog.

There's Nothing my mom can't do Something with.

She even rescued a rusty old truck, on its way to the scrapyard.

The truck was too big to carry to the fourteenth floor, so we kept it out back and planted it with grasses and daisies. Mom said it would soon be whistling and rustling just like the distant prairies.

One day, Mom saw an abandoned
boat she simply had to have.

That boat sure was heavy!

BIG SALLY

We said hello to Mr. Price as usual, and he said
"Harumph!"

But this time, that wasn't all he said.

"There she goes again,"
he said. "Your mom won't
be satisfied until she's
changed every last thing
in the world!"

That night, I started to wonder.
I started to worry. What if Mr Price
was right? There was nothing in
our flat Mum hadn't changed.

Or, rather, there was ONE thing . . .

ME!

What if Mom wanted to change me too?

What if she wanted me this way?

Or that way?

Or another way altogether?

I had to leave. I had to go far, far away.

I knew the very place.

It was cold in the prairies. I curled up and listened to the rustling, the whistling, and the warbling. And I thought how much I missed my must-have mom.

The grasses swirled and swished. And when they parted . . .

Mom was there! And she'd brought breakfast.

We warmed our hands on our teacups and I told Mom all about Mr. Price and the worries that had come in the night.

And here's what Mom said to me.

"Jake," she said. "There's not a single thing about you that I would ever change. You'll go changing anyway, without any help from me. You'll grow like the trees and blossom like the flowers. You'll shine just like the sun. All I'm going to do is stand by and watch.

And I'm going to love every minute!"

And my must-have mom told me and told me again
that I was her one and only must-have son!